JON BLAKE

Illustrations by Martin Chatterton

WALKER BOOKS
AND SUBSIDIARIES

LONDON ◆ BOSTON ◆ SYDNEY

AV
/SF/C   C706971999

First published 1995 by
Walker Books Ltd, 87 Vauxhall Walk
London SE11 5HJ

Text © 1995 Jon Blake
Illustrations © 1995 Martin Chatterton

This book has been typeset in Garamond.

Printed in England by Clays Ltd, St Ives plc

British Library Cataloguing in Publication Data
A catalogue record for this book
is available from the British Library.

ISBN 0-7445-4104-2

CONTENTS

PART 1

In a huge stadium, somewhere on Earth, the Great Stupendo was about to perform his latest stunt.

A hush fell over the crowd. The Great Stupendo revved up his bike.

He sped down the track like a bullet.

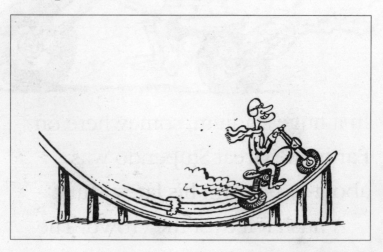

He raced up the ramp like wildfire.

He flew into the air like a jet plane.

High over the cars he sailed.

Then SMASH!

He crashed to the ground,
bounced off his bike, and ripped his
trousers.

Everyone cheered wildly. Everyone, that is, except the Great Stupendo's daughter, Little Stupendo.

After the show, the Stupendos went home. As usual, the Great Stupendo took a nap. He took his motorbike with him, because he always slept with his motorbike.

Little Stupendo sulked. She wished she could sleep with a motorbike. In fact, she secretly wished she could do stunts as well. It was much more interesting than mending trousers.

Little Stupendo
went into the yard.
She climbed the
shed and pretended
it was a skyscraper.

She trained the
cat and pretended
it was a tiger.

Then she peeped
over at next door's
washing line.

I could pretend
that was a
high wire.

Mr Chinspot lived next door. He
was a tall, thin, suspicious old man.
He preferred to be left in peace
with his matchstick models.

"What is it now?" he grumbled.

Suddenly there was a loud scream. It came from the Stupendos' house.

Little Stupendo went hurrying back inside with Mr Chinspot following. They found the Great Stupendo in the bathroom, shaking all over.

Little Stupendo hardly dared look. Was it a snake? A scorpion? A sewer rat?

Actually, it was none of these things. It was a tiny, harmless, frightened spider. Little Stupendo put a tooth-mug over it and slid a postcard under it. Then she threw it out of the window.

The Great Stupendo calmed down. He turned to Mr Chinspot with a solemn warning: "No one else must ever know about my secret fear," he said.

PART 2

A week passed. Then it was time for
the Great Stupendo's next stunt.
For this he needed a barrel, so he
went off to Barrels-R-Us to buy one.
Little Stupendo went too. She had
shopping of her own to do.

Near the shops, they saw a poster
which made the Great Stupendo's
teeth gnash together:

See the one and only

Johnny Bravo

DRIVE through a hoop of fire on a lawnmower! WRESTLE a man-eating hippopotamus and BUNGEE-JUMP from Cloud-Jabber Tower in a one-and-only STUNT SPECTACULAR **this SATURDAY!**

The Great Stupendo looked both ways, then drew glasses on Johnny Bravo, and scribbled RUBBISH all over the poster.

Johnny Bravo, as you may have guessed, was the Great Stupendo's greatest rival.

Still sulking, the Great Stupendo
went into Barrels-R-Us. "I want a
barrel," he grunted. "Please," he added.

The saleswoman nodded. "Is that
a barrel for beer?" she asked. "Or for
rainwater?"

"It is a barrel," replied the Great
Stupendo, "for myself."

The Great Stupendo measured
himself against the barrels till he
found one big enough to curl up in.

Back home, the Great Stupendo began to climb into the barrel. Then he had a nasty thought:

What if there's a spider in the barrel?

The Great Stupendo shuddered. He called for Little Stupendo, but Little Stupendo was still out shopping. There was only one person he could ask for help – Mr Chinspot.

As usual, Mr Chinspot was
working on a matchstick model.
He wasn't at all happy to be
disturbed.

"Could you please
climb into this
barrel?" asked the
Great Stupendo.

Mr Chinspot
was suspicious.
"What for?" he
grunted.

"To check
there are no ...
things in it,"
replied the
Great Stupendo.

I hope this isn't some kind of trick.

The Great Stupendo fetched a
chair. Mr Chinspot got onto it and,
with some difficulty, climbed into
the barrel.

The Great Stupendo went off to
change. Mr Chinspot peered about
in the dim light. It was hard even to
see his own feet.

Meanwhile, a van arrived outside.
Two workmen got out and went
into the Great Stupendo's house.

They fitted the lid on the barrel
and carried it off to their van.

Mr Chinspot didn't know what
was going on. He banged and he
shouted, but no one seemed to hear.

Suddenly he felt himself moving,
very fast.

Then he heard the sound of an
excited crowd.

Next he seemed to be floating,
quite calmly and gently.

"Actually," he thought to himself,
"this is quite pleasant."

Next second...

The crowd went berserk as the
barrel was brought to shore.

Suddenly, however, the cheers stopped, and there was a stunned silence. The man in the barrel was not the Great Stupendo!

Mr Chinspot dusted himself down, shook himself out, and frowned a deadly frown.

And with that, Mr Chinspot vowed to get his revenge.

PART 3

Next day, the Great Stupendo
went to see Vanessa Gabble, his
agent. Vanessa was the person who
organized the stunts.

Vanessa looked worried. She
showed a newspaper to the Great
Stupendo.

The next newspaper was

even worse.

"There is only one thing for it," said Vanessa. "We must make sure your next stunt is so fantastic that Johnny Bravo can never follow it."

"But what shall I do?" asked the Great Stupendo.

Vanessa showed the Great
Stupendo a photo. It was a picture
of a mighty canyon – Vulture
Canyon, a hundred metres wide
and four kilometres deep.

The Great Stupendo gasped.

That was a truly scary thought,
even for the Great Stupendo.

Back at home, the Great
Stupendo began to practise.

First he put a
plank between
two chairs
and walked
across that.

Then he put a
broomstick
between two
step-ladders.

"Now I need something more
difficult," he said to himself.

Out in the yard, Little Stupendo
was putting up a new clothes line.

Little Stupendo wasn't very pleased
when the Great Stupendo got up
on her new line. He even used her
clothes-line pole for balance. He
practised all day, till the sun went
down, then went off to bed with his
motorbike.

"I'll show him," said Little Stupendo to herself.

As the Great Stupendo snored in his bed, Little Stupendo walked the plank. Then the broomstick. By the light of the moon, she crept outside and climbed onto the clothes line. Bit by bit, she learned how to keep her balance. She even waved to the crowd, except no one was watching.

No one, that is, except Mr Chinspot.

Little Stupendo almost fell off the line. Then she saw it was only her old neighbour.

Mr Chinspot's brain began to tick over. A plan formed in his mind. It was the plan for his revenge.

Next day, Mr Chinspot paid a visit to 333 Sunset Villas.

333 Sunset Villas was the home of Johnny Bravo.

Mr Chinspot rang the bell.

As usual, Johnny Bravo was riding his bike round the house. The bike had two huge mirrors, so Johnny could watch himself everywhere he went.

Johnny bumped down the stairs, did a wheelie through the hall and almost made Mr Chinspot jump out of his socks.

Mr Chinspot leaned closer and
whispered in Johnny Bravo's ear.
A big, broad smile spread across
Johnny's face.

PART 4

At last it was the morning of the
great event. All was dim and still
and silent at Vulture Canyon. Then,
as if from nowhere, a helicopter
appeared.

In the helicopter
were Mr Chinspot
and Johnny Bravo.

A rope-ladder
came out of the
helicopter. Down
the ladder climbed
Johnny Bravo.
Johnny was doing
something to the
high wire.
Something he
wasn't supposed
to be doing.

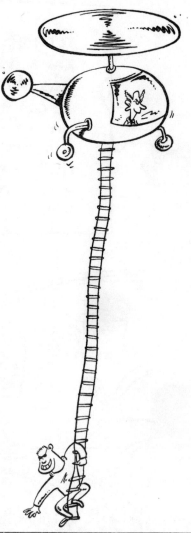

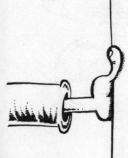

Perhaps you think you know what Johnny Bravo was doing. If so, write it on a postcard, stick on a first class stamp and send it to yourself. That way you won't spoil it for anyone else.

Dawn broke. People began to arrive. They came in their cars, their trucks and their caravans. They came on their bikes, their skateboards and their space-hoppers. Some even came on their feet.

The Great Stupendo appeared from his caravan. At first Little Stupendo walked alongside him. Soon, though, the Great Stupendo was swallowed up in a crowd of reporters, supporters and TV cameras.

Little Stupendo watched anxiously as the Great Stupendo reached the very edge of the canyon. All round the world, on a million tellies, others were watching as well.

Silence fell. The Great Stupendo took his first step. There was a little wobble. The Great Stupendo took a deep breath, steadied himself, and edged out over the mighty canyon. So far, so good.

The Great Stupendo moved faster. With every step he became more confident. Soon he was halfway across.
And then…
he stopped…
stopped dead.

"Come on, Great Stupendo!" cried a voice in the crowd.

But the Great Stupendo would not move another inch.

Whispers went round the crowd:

Suddenly there was a great commotion. A little figure fought her way to the front of the crowd. In her hands was an old washing-line pole.

They were too late. Little
Stupendo had reached the high
wire. She balanced the pole in her
hands and took two shaky steps
onto the wire.

But Little Stupendo had practised
hard. She fixed her eyes straight
ahead and planted her footsteps
perfectly. Soon she was moving as
smoothly as a mountain goat.

The Great Stupendo nervously
turned his head. He could not

She's almost as good as the Great Stupendo!